The UNDER DOGS

SERVE
IT UP

RAZORBILL

An imprint of
Penguin Random House LLC, New York

To Arlo, Clancy, and their
faithful hound Wicket, the best
ball dog around! —KT & JT

For Charlie, Annie, and Frankie —SG

First published as *The Underdogs Hit a Grand Slam*
in Australia by Hardie Grant Children's Publishing in 2022
Published in the United States of America by Razorbill,
an imprint of Penguin Random House LLC, 2023
Text copyright © 2022 by Kate and Jol Temple
Illustrations copyright © 2022 by Shiloh Gordon
Activities text copyright © 2023 by Penguin Random House LLC

Razorbill & colophon are registered
trademarks of Penguin Random House LLC.
The Penguin colophon is a registered
trademark of Penguin Books Limited.

Visit us online at penguinrandomhouse.com.

Library of Congress Cataloging-in-Publication Data
Names: Temple, Kate, author. | Temple, Jol, author. | Gordon,
Shiloh, illustrator. | Title: The underdogs serve it up /
Kate and Jol Temple ; art by Shiloh Gordon. | Description:
New York: Razorbill, 2022. | Series: The Underdogs |
"First published in Australia by Hardie Grant Children's
Publishing in 2022." | Audience: Ages 6–9 years. | Summary:
In their latest case, the Underdogs must fetch the identity
of a tennis ball thief. Identifiers: LCCN 2022032699 (print)
| LCCN 2022032700 (ebook) | ISBN 9780593527009 (trade
paperback) | ISBN 9780593527016 (epub) | Subjects: CYAC:
Dogs–Fiction. | Cats–Fiction. | Tennis–Fiction. | Mystery and
detective stories. | Humorous stories. | LCGFT: Detective
and mystery fiction. | Humorous fiction. | Animal fiction. |
Classification: LCC PZ7.T246 Uo 2022 (print) | LCC PZ7.T246
(ebook) | DDC [Fic]–dc23 | LC record available at https://lccn.
loc.gov/2022032699 | LC ebook record available at https://
lccn.loc.gov/2022032700
ISBN 9780593527009

Printed in the United States of America
1st Printing

LSCH

Series design by Sarah Mitchell

The publisher does not have any control over
and does not assume any responsibility for
author or third-party websites or their content.

KATE AND JOL TEMPLE

The UNDER DOGS

SERVE IT UP

ART BY
SHILOH
GORDON

RAZORBILL

Here we are again, mystery lovers. In the office of Dogtown's second-best (or first-worst) detectives— **the Underdogs!**

It's a day like any other... well, not quite. There's a **funny** smell about. A **very** funny smell.

What's that smell?

That dog sniffing the air, that's Barkley. He's been an **Underdog detective** for quite a while, so he's used to sniffing out trouble, and right now, something sure smells **strange**.

That's Fang. She's not a dog, she's a cat—and the only cat in the **UNDERDOG DETECTIVE AGENCY**.

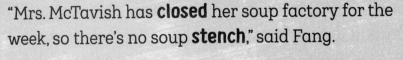

"Mrs. McTavish has **closed** her soup factory for the week, so there's no soup **stench**," said Fang.

Mrs. McTavish is the **downstairs** neighbor. There are two things you need to know about her; she's a terrier and she makes soup—very **STINKY** soup. What flavor was she cooking last week? Oh, that's right... asparagus and boiled egg. **YUCK!**

"Why would she close her factory?" asked Fang suspiciously. Fang is **always** suspicious. That's what makes her a **great** Underdog.

That's Carl, the Chihuahua Underdog who looks like he's doing some important detective paperwork... **NOT!**

"Mrs. McTavish **plays** tennis?" asked Fang.

"No. She has a food truck!" replied Carl.

MRS. MCTAVISH SETS UP
FOOD TRUCK AT GRAND SLAM

SOUP

DOGTOWN
GRAND SLAM

MENU
DOG

Fang shook her head. "I don't know why everyone's so **excited** about the Grand Slam. It's just a **bunch** of dogs chasing balls around."

"Exactly!" said Carl and Barkley.

"That's why everyone **loves** tennis!" added Barkley. "And the Grand Slam is the **BIGGEST** tennis tournament in Dogtown."

It's true. Every dog in Dogtown loves tennis. And no one loves it **more** than Carl. The crowds! The tennis stars! The tennis balls! Carl had been **counting down** the days until the Grand Slam started and now it was finally here. He even put **pictures** up of all the stars.

"I'd sure **love** to go to the Grand Slam," said Carl. "This is going to be the **best** one yet! How cool would it be to see Barry Barker play!"

"If he wins, he'll **break** the Dogtown **record** set by the great Bjorn Dawg!" added Barkley.

"Who's Bjorn Dawg?" asked Fang.

"He's only the **GREATEST** tennis dog of all time!" said Carl. "He's retired from tennis and is a **sports commentator** now."

All this tennis talk was getting too **exciting** for Carl, who had started **playing** air tennis with a flyswatter.

Can we get some tickets, Barkley? CAN WE?

10

Barkley looked doubtful. "I **wish** we could. Maybe next year, Carl. Right now our **bank account** isn't looking too healthy ... and those Grand Slam tickets sure are **expensive!**"

Carl pulled his **best** puppy-dog eyes.

"Haven't you got some **REAL** work to do?" Barkley said.

"I've got **REAL** work to do!" said Dr. Spots.

That's Dr. Spots. She's the **brains** of this operation. More brains than spots, or maybe it's the other way around? What **outrageous** inventions has she been working on today? A doggy raincoat that **doubles** as a life vest? A bionic stick launcher? A rubber-chicken toy that squeaks in **fourteen** different languages?

Spots looked up. "I'm working on my **automatic ball-fetching machine**. It will revolutionize trips to the dog park … if I can **just** get it working!"

Yep. Good old Spots, tinkering away on another machine that **DOESN'T WORK**.

Barkley shook his head. The sad truth was there was no **REAL** work to do. It had been **way** too long since their last **REAL** case and if they didn't get one soon, this detective agency was going to the dogs... **or worse**.

That's when there was a **knock** at the door. Carl
stopped pretending to hit tennis balls.

KNOCK!
KNOCK!

16

They didn't often get **knocks** on the door. Carl was very confused. He thought it might be the start of a funny **knock-knock** joke.

"Who's there?"

"The door, Carl."

"The door Carl who?"

"The door, Carl! Open the door!"

"Ha ha! That's a good one, Fang. Wait... I don't get it."

While Carl was **scratching** his head, Fang **opened** the door. She smiled her **toothy** smile and gave her best detective-agency introduction.

Welcome to the Underdog Detective Agency, no clue left undug!

Now who do you **suppose** was in the doorway? A poodle in a fancy hat? A Pomeranian graphic designer?

No. It was a **hedgehog**, a blue **bow** in her spikes and a **handkerchief** clenched in her little paws.

Help me, Underdogs! You have to find my husband! He's vanished!

BETTY HENSON:
- Not an echidna
- Not a porcupine
- Still very spiky

The small, **spiky** hedgehog shuffled in, followed by two **smaller** hedgehogs. They were just about the **cutest** things you've ever seen. **EVER.**

"Hello, pups!" said Carl.

We aren't called pups. Little hedgehogs are called hoglets.

Hoglets! Aww! That's even cuter!

The big hedgehog introduced herself. Her name was Betty Henson. Her little **hoglets** were Ben and Barb. And their dad? His name was Benson, and by the sound of it, he was **missing**.

Now, missing hedgehog cases don't **waddle** in every day, so naturally the Underdogs **jumped** at the chance to **help**.

"So, when did you last see your husband?"

"He went to work two days ago … and I haven't seen him since!"

"Hmm, suspicious. And what does your husband do for work, Betty?"

"He's in pest control."

"Interesting. I hear that's a **good** line of work for hedgehogs," said Barkley.

"That's true. No one gets rid of ants **faster** than a hedgehog," Betty replied.

"Pest control, you say? Right. And where was he **working** on the day he **disappeared**?" asked Fang.

"At the Dogtown Tennis Center," said Betty.

All their **ears** pricked up. Maybe they would get to see the Grand Slam after all!

"That's what she said, Carl," **growled** Barkley.

"But that's where they're **playing** the Dogtown Grand Slam!" said Carl.

"We know! Now, if you don't mind, I have some **detective questions** to ask Betty," said Barkley.

"Why would they **need** pest control at the Grand Slam?" asked Fang.

"International tennis players are **very fussy**," replied Betty. "Any **fleas** or **ticks** and there's trouble!"

"Makes sense," said Barkley. "We **can't** have the Dogtown Tennis Center full of fleas or cockroaches. Imagine what they'd say in the newspapers!"

Betty **sniffed** into her handkerchief. Fang handed her a tissue.

"Really?" replied Fang. "Well, that's just great! **CASE CLOSED!**"

"Of course I **don't know** where he is!" snapped Betty. "If I knew, I wouldn't be here."

"Good point," said Fang. "Let me ask **another** question. Is there anyone who **doesn't** like Benson?"

"Everyone likes Benson! Have you **ever** met someone who doesn't like hedgehogs?"

Barkley and Fang looked at each other. She had made another good point. **EVERYONE** likes hedgehogs.

Betty continued, "Benson was the **kindest** hedgehog around. He wouldn't hurt a fly. Well, he might **eat** a fly, but you know what I mean..."

Barkley **scratched** his head … he didn't have fleas, he was just thinking. Fang **scratched** her head, too, but she did have fleas. This was all very curious.

So, we have a missing hedgehog and no lead?

"Hedgehogs don't wear leads! Or collars! Or any of that other **doggy fashion** for that matter," sobbed Betty.

Barkley stood up. Enough **chitchat**. It was time to get to work.

"Well, Betty, you've come to the right place. We might not have **much** to go on, but the Underdogs are on the case and we'll find your **spiky** husband. He probably just got **stuck** on something."

"And ninety-nine percent of missing hedgehog cases end **very** well," added Fang.

"What about the other one percent?" asked Betty.

They end with ice cream!

"I have just **one** more question before we get started…" said Barkley. Something was **bugging** him, and when a detective has an itch, they have to **scratch** it, especially if that detective is a dog.

"What made you choose the Underdogs? Was it our **fine reputation** for cracking cases?"

"No."

"Maybe you'd **read** about us in the newspaper?"

"No."

"Why **DID** you choose the Underdogs to crack the case?" asked Barkley.

"Well, the Top Dogs are very busy. I had **no choice** but to come to you." Betty shrugged.

The Underdogs sighed.

Do you know who the Top Dogs are? Of course you do. Everyone does. They're the **number-one** detectives in Dogtown. A **flashy** brother-sister team of Weimaraners with fast cars, a helicopter, and even their own TV show!

Barkley shook his head. No matter how **hard** the Underdogs tried, the Top Dogs just kept getting all the cases. Was there **anything** those Top Dogs couldn't do?

"I guess they're busy solving **all** the cases in Dogtown…" said Fang.

CHAPTER 3

After showing Betty and her hoglets out, Fang and Barkley put their heads together. Well, they didn't **LITERALLY** put their heads together because Barkley was pretty sure Fang had **fleas**.

Something smells fishy. And this time it's not the soup factory.

I know what you mean. Why would a pest controller go missing from the Grand Slam . . . it doesn't make sense.

Fang **paced** the room. It's a thing cats do. Dogs only do it if they're about to have a sleep (or a poo), and Barkley was **wide-awake** and…well…he'd get around to that **other** business later!

And **WHY** are baby hedgehogs called hoglets? It sounds made-up. Although, they sure were cute.

Barkley looked out the window, but all he could see was a bus driving by with a **big** ad for the Grand Slam and guess who was on it? Yup, that's right, the Top Dogs.

"We have to **solve** this case, and fast. Otherwise, we'll never get another case, not while the Top Dogs are so **famous**," said Fang.

"It's time we made a name for ourselves, but not for **hitting** balls, or having our own TV show, and not for wearing **fancy** clothes and having **heaps** of fans…" said Barkley.

"Aww, drat," said Carl.

"No," continued Barkley. "We need to make a name for ourselves by **solving cases**! Good old-fashioned detective work. Underdogs, it's time to **find** a missing echidna!"

Ah, he's a hedgehog, Barkley.

That's what I meant. We need to get to the tennis center and find this porcupine.

While Barkley was giving his little speech, Spots had been working on a **project** of her own.

"So, if the last place Benson Henson was seen was the Dogtown Tennis Center, you're going to **need** to get down there and **find** some clues. And I've got just the thing for you."

Fang's ears perked up. Fang **loved** a gadget.

"OOOH! Is it a recording device hidden in a tennis shoe?"

"No."

Fang felt a bit **silly** wearing the headband. Barkley felt a **LOT** silly wearing the short shorts, but going undercover was all in a day's work.

"It's a nice day outside," added Dr. Spots. "Why don't you go **walkies** to the Dogtown Tennis Center?"

"WALKIES?" Fang shook her head. "Cats don't do walkies. No way ... we're taking the **scooter**."

Dr. Spots and Barkley looked **sheepish**. That doesn't mean they looked like sheep, it means there was **NO SCOOTER!**

"What happened to our scooter?" meowed Fang.

"Ahhhh, we sold it," grumbled Barkley. "Times are tough, Fang, and **fancy** scooters cost money."

"But don't worry, we **swapped** it for something pretty cool," added Dr. Spots. "And I've even made some **impressive** modifications."

Fang followed Barkley and Dr. Spots down to the parking lot, but all they saw was a **tricycle** with a **frilly** umbrella.

"I've put a secret **tracking device** in the handlebars," said Dr. Spots, handing Fang a microchip the size of a **pea**.

After all, they were going to need **more** than an umbrella and a clunky old tricycle to crack this case!

CHAPTER 4

Fang **loved** being a detective, even if it meant she was dressed in tennis gear and riding a tricycle through the streets of Dogtown. There was **nothing** quite like it. She loved the clues, the mystery, and best of all—she loved **cracking** a case.

As cases go, this was a **big** one. A missing hedgehog and father of those two cute hoglets! Fang was determined to **find** Benson Henson, and fast. Barkley felt the same way. He always gave every case his **very best**, and when it came to a missing hedgehog, the clock was **ticking**.

Benson could be anywhere! But they would start where Benson was last seen, the Dogtown Tennis Center. Their plan was to **sniff out** some clues and see what turned up.

Barkley pedaled as fast as his dog legs would let him. They **swerved** and **steered** through the busy streets, passing movie theaters and shops, and the **fancy** dog hotels where sleeping dogs lie.

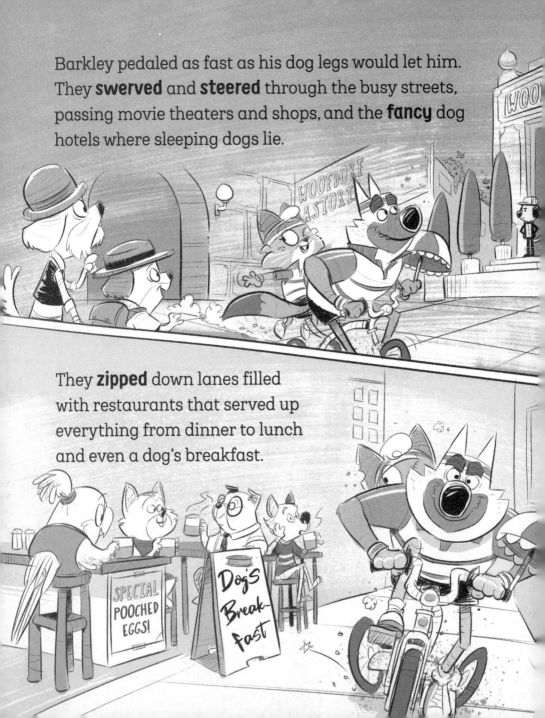

WOOFDORF ASTORIA

WOO

They **zipped** down lanes filled with restaurants that served up everything from dinner to lunch and even a dog's breakfast.

SPECIAL POOCHED EGGS!

Dog's Break-fast

They took a **shortcut** through the flower market, down a street, left, then right, then left again, took a dogleg through the park (not an actual dogleg), and **popped** out right in front of the tennis center.

This is it!

It was indeed. Dogtown Tennis Center. Home of the Grand Slam.

Outside the tennis courts, excited tennis fans were **already** beginning to roll up. Fang and Barkley **parked** the tricycle and looked around. There were ticket stands and stalls selling **T-shirts** and **snacks**.

"There's Mrs. McTavish's food truck!" said Fang.

Barkley looked over. Fang was right. What was she serving up today? Sardine and cabbage soup. **STINKY!**

"Maybe we should start looking for **clues** over here," growled Barkley, holding his **nose**.

"Wait," whispered Fang. "We don't have **tickets**." It was true. Every dog in the line had a ticket in their paw.

"We can talk our way in," said Barkley.

But talking wouldn't do much **good** this time because when they got to the front of the line, there was no one to talk to. Just a ticket machine. **BEEP!**

Fang tried scanning her bus pass. But the gate **wouldn't** open.

Fang pointed a **paw** toward a security gate.

CENTER COURT

SECTION K9

PLAYERS ONLY

What about over there?

Why do all security dogs have to be so grumpy looking?! Still, Fang and Barkley had a few **tricks** up their sleeves.

With their **headbands** on, Fang and Barkley **strutted** up to the security gates.

"Act like a **tennis player**," whispered Barkley.

"How do we do that?" asked Fang.

"Um … maybe we do a few **stretches**?"

"Welcome, players. Please come in—hold on!" said the security dog. "You're a cat."

"Tell me **something** I don't know." Fang smiled.

Cats don't play tennis.

"Sure we do," said Fang. "Actually, we're a team. The first dog-and-cat **doubles** team. And we're **pretty good**. Isn't that right, Barkley?"

Barkley nodded. "We sure are, partner. Now we need to **hit** the court and get warmed up for our **BIG** match."

The sausage dog frowned and then she **laughed**.

A dog-and-cat team? I get it, you're the halftime entertainment! Classic.

That isn't what Fang meant, but if this **grumbly** security guard wanted to think so, that was just fine, so long as she **opened** the gate and let them through, which she did.

"Nice work, Fang," said Barkley. "Now let's **snoop** around and find Benson Henson."

PLAYERS
LY

Fang and Barkley **walked** up a set of stairs into the tennis center. On center court were two dogs getting ready for their match. Around the court, a team of Jack Russell **ball dogs** looked on, waiting for the match to start.

If you don't know what a ball dog is, let me fill you in. A ball dog has a very **important** job: every time the ball gets hit out of bounds, they need to **run and grab it**. And when it comes to **chasing** balls, no dog is better than a Jack Russell.

Just then, **someone** caught Fang's eye…

"Look!" hissed Fang. She **pointed** to one of the players. "I know him! That's that famous tennis dog Barry Barker!"

Fang was right, it sure was. The **number-one** player in Dogtown. And he was about to play another famous tennis star … **ASH BARKY.**

"Welcome to the Dogtown Grand Slam!" said a commentator over the **loudspeaker**—an English cocker spaniel by the name of Eddie Yapstick, and next to Eddie Yapstick sat a golden retriever with a **microphone**.

The match is about to get started and it should be a good one!

EDDIE + BJORN:
- Love tennis
- Great at interrupting others
- Use expensive microphones

Barkley recognized the golden retriever straightaway. That was Bjorn Dawg! The one Carl had a **picture** of on the wall. The **greatest** tennis player *OF ALL TIME*.

Barkley and Fang **snuck** into a pair of empty seats. Fang was scanning the crowd, looking for any **sign** of a hedgehog. Barkley was a bit distracted by the match... something was **wrong**.

A Jack Russell ran out onto center court with an **empty** ball bucket and a **horrified** look on his face.

Here's the head ball dog, Jack Russell.

A Jack Russell called Jack Russell?

CHAPTER 5

The crowd **gasped**. The tennis players looked confused.
The ball dogs raced around **madly** looking for balls.

Right then a **schnauzer** in a little jacket came **dashing** onto the court.

Here's Steffi Gruff! She's the dog in charge of the Grand Slam. Maybe she will find some tennis balls?

STEFFI GRUFF:
- In charge of Grand Slam
- Wears little jackets
- Loves the Top Dogs

Fang and Barkley joined the **hunt**. Now all the dogs on the court were looking for balls. They sniffed **under** seats. No balls. They sniffed on **top** of the umpire. No balls. They sniffed **everywhere**!

It was true. No one could **find** a single tennis ball anywhere. That's when Steffi Gruff took the microphone and said the words **every** Underdog dreams of hearing...

OK, not those words, the **next** ones...

Now, it's not very often that a detective is there **exactly** when you need them. Usually, they turn up afterward when the case is getting cold. Not this time. The case was **hotter** than apple pie on a summer's day and the Underdogs were right there to **scoop** it up.

Barkley and Fang raced over and **jumped** on court.

"You're in luck, we're the Underdogs. No clue left undug," announced Barkley.

"Who?" said Steffi Gruff.

The Underdogs, you've probably heard of us. We're detectives.

The schnauzer had **no idea** who they were, but she was happy to get any **help** she could.

"We can help you **crack** the case of the missing balls. Now tell us everything," said Barkley.

Steffi Gruff started talking. The tennis balls had been there last night, she'd seen them with her **own** eyes! But now they were **gone**. Every last one!

"Without the tennis balls, there is **NO** Grand Slam!" Steffi said.

"Can you help find them?" cried Steffi.

Barkley was just about to tell Steffi that they **absolutely** could. After all, they were detectives, really great detectives. But just then, a dark Weimaraner-shaped shadow **fell** over them and **blocked** out the sun. Barkley and Fang looked up.

The Top Dogs.

"We hear someone's **stolen** all the tennis balls. This sounds like a case for..."

"The Underdogs!" interrupted Fang.

"Who?" said the Top Dogs, **lowering** their sunglasses.

"We're detectives," snapped Fang.

The Top Dogs looked at each other and started to **laugh**.

"Nice try, cat."

The Weimaraners turned back to Steffi. "Don't worry, we'll get **all** the balls back ... just in time for us to **win** the Grand Slam."

The Top Dogs gave each other a **high four**.

Fang's fur bristled, which means it stood on end so she looked like a **scrubbing brush**. That happened when she was scared or when she didn't like someone. And right now, she wasn't **scared**.

"I think we have enough **information** to go on," said one of the Top Dogs.

Barkley coughed. It was one of those **fake coughs** to get some attention. No one gave him any, so he just went ahead and **said** what he was thinking.

How do you plan on finding the ball thief if you don't have ANY clues? Don't you need to ask a few questions?

Fang nodded. It made sense, but the Top Dogs just **laughed**. One of those **annoying** laughs dogs do when they think they're **smarter** than you.

"When you're as good as we are, you don't **need** clues," said the first Top Dog.

"Clues just get in the way of **cracking** the case," agreed the second Top Dog.

Barkley rolled his eyes and whispered to Fang.

This is when they start saying how great they are . . .

"Did I mention how **great** we are?"

Barkley was just about to say that they definitely had, but the two Weimaraners had already **spun** on their tails and raced off, **leaping** over the net in one bound and giving each other **ANOTHER** high four.

"Wow. We're lucky the Top Dogs are on the case," said Steffi Gruff.

Fang didn't think it was so great the Top Dogs were on the case and Barkley **REALLY** didn't think it was so great. What kind of detective doesn't need clues?

This was their chance to solve not one but **TWO CASES!** After all, the Top Dogs didn't know it wasn't just the balls that had gone missing ... there was also a missing hedgehog!

Were the cases connected? If so, how? And who were the suspects? These were **good** questions. Detective questions. And if the Top Dogs thought they could solve the case without asking **any** questions, well, that suited Barkley just fine. It meant more **clues** for the Underdogs.

But they needed to find a **suspect**, and fast. Lucky for them, one was right behind them ...

CHAPTER 6

Steffi Gruff **smiled** into the distance, watching as the Top Dogs disappeared.

"Gee, those two are something!" Steffi said.

"Excuse me," interrupted Barkley, "but before we get started, I just have **one** question for you..."

Steffi turned and looked at Barkley in surprise.

Oh, you're still here!

"Yes, we are and we're going to **crack** this case."

"You probably don't need to **worry** about that now that the Top Dogs are on the case. They're the greatest," said Steffi.

"So they keep telling us ..." grumbled Barkley. "But I still have one question ... who has the **key** to the storeroom?"

"Just me and ..."

Fang **scratched** her fur. There was something suspicious about Bjorn Dawg ... but she couldn't put her paw on it.

"Mind if we take a look at your key, Mr. Dawg?" said Fang. But when Bjorn Dawg **opened** up a drawer in his desk, the key was **gone**!

"OK, that's enough commentating, you two."

News flash! The big dog is getting serious.

Very serious . . .

"Cut it out."

News flash! He wants us to cut it out.

Choppy-chop-chop!

News flash! Now he's shaking his head!

Shake, doggy! Shake!

Barkley and Fang turned to Steffi. Maybe she would be more help!

"Do you think you could **show** us to the storeroom where the balls were last seen?" said Fang.

Steffi nodded and led the Underdogs to a **hallway** next to the court. At the end of the hallway was the **storeroom**. How did they know it was the storeroom? It said so.

Inside was a **large** room with all sorts of sports gear, spare rackets, rolled-up tennis nets, and two big **empty** ball bins.

"This is where we keep all the balls," said Steffi. Fang looked around. It was all pretty standard except for a table with **cake** and **snacks**.

Yum!

That's for the tennis players!

Barkley and Fang took their time **combing** the room. That doesn't mean they actually used a comb; it means they **poked around**, looking for any clues. The room had no windows and only one door, which meant that the ball thief must have come through the door.

"I don't suppose you have any **security cameras** in here?" asked Barkley, but Steffi shook her head.

"I think there is one in the hallway though," said Steffi.
"But we **don't** really use it."

"Still, it might have **caught** someone leaving the area,"
said Barkley. "Let's have a look."

Steffi and the Underdogs went back out into the hallway and looked around. Sure enough, up in a **dusty** corner was an old security camera!

95

"I think it's broken," said Steffi, pointing to a big **crack** running down the lens.

"Don't worry," said Barkley. "We'll get Dr. Spots to take a look at it and see if there's any **evidence**."

But the crack was not their **biggest** problem... The dusty corner was full of cobwebs, and a really big **spider** had made her home right on the camera with a million of her friends, too.

"Where's that pest controller when you need him!" grumbled Steffi, **wiping** the cobwebs out of the way.

Pest controller? Barkley and Fang looked at each other. Did she mean Benson Henson? The **missing** echidna? Sorry—hedgehog! Fang's fur stood on end. Clues were flying thick and fast.

BENSON HENSON!

"When was the last time you saw the pest controller?" asked Barkley.

"Come to think of it," said Steffi, "it was just before the balls went missing! Do you think he **stole** them?"

"Let's not **jump** to any conclusions. Only good detective work can answer that," said Barkley.

Steffi shook her head. She pulled out her mobile phone and **spun** through her contacts until she found Benson Henson.

They all waited.

"He's not answering ..." said Steffi.

Somewhere someone was **playing** music. Fang recognized the tune straightaway. It was the **Catchy Dog Song** and it was getting louder. Who was playing that?!

Fang **loved** this song! And by the looks of it, so did Steffi! Her foot started **tapping**, her tail was **wagging**, and the next thing she knew, they were **dancing** up a storm.

"**STOP!**" barked Barkley. "That sound is coming from the storeroom!" The Underdogs **raced** back in and what did they find at the **bottom** of the ball bin?

Benson Henson's cell phone! Their first **clue**.

This was all **very** suspicious. But Steffi didn't have time for this. She had a stadium full of spectators that were getting very **upset**. The sound of their **growls** and **grumbles** were getting **louder** and **louder**. She needed tennis balls... and fast!

"It sounds like the **hedgehog** did it," said Steffi.

"But…" said Fang.

"No buts. You need to find him and the tennis balls. How **long** will that take?" asked Steffi, looking at her watch again. "If I don't get this match **started** soon, I don't know **what** will happen!"

The Underdogs followed Steffi back out to center court. She was right. The crowd was restless and the tennis stars were very, **VERY** annoyed.

"I've got an **idea**," said Fang brightly. "The tennis balls might have gone missing, but I think I saw a soccer ball in the storeroom. Why don't you play the **first match** with a soccer ball?" said Fang.

"YOU CAN'T PLAY **TENNIS** WITH A **SOCCER** BALL!" yelled Steffi.

The sound of the annoyed crowd was getting **louder**.

Steffi looked at the **angry** crowd and the even **angrier** tennis stars. "Fine, we'll try it. It will buy me some time to send out Jack Russell to **chase** down a delivery of tennis balls!"

I'm on it! If there's a ball out there, I'll find it.

With that, the Dogtown Tennis Grand Slam went ahead... but with a **soccer ball**! Barry Barker did his best to serve it, but it was too heavy. Ash Barky tried to hit it back but ended up **bouncing** it off her head.

After **five** broken rackets, it was clear that the soccer ball wasn't working. So, what do you think they did next while they were **waiting** for Jack Russell to find tennis balls somewhere in Dogtown? Yup. You guessed it. They tried some other balls!

"This **isn't** working!" barked Steffi. She was just about to say, "Where is that Jack Russell?" when who should come racing back into the stadium? **JACK RUSSELL!**

"Thank dog you're back!" said Steffi. "But **where** are the tennis balls?"

"You're **not** going to believe this, Steffi," panted Jack Russell. His face was pink with exhaustion. His paws were **covered** in dirt and he **smelled** dreadful!

Wow. You look like you've run a marathon!

I went to every sports shop in Dogtown! I looked in every drain! And there's no tennis balls anywhere! Someone has stolen all the tennis balls in Dogtown!

It was true; without balls the Grand Slam would **have** to be **canceled**! The players were upset! The crowd was upset! They **thumped** their tails and **howled** in disappointment.

The **only** thing that seemed to make anyone feel better was when the Top Dogs came **bounding** back onto center court.

"Don't worry, everyone. We've **almost** cracked the case," said the first Top Dog.

"We'll have this **ball thief** wrapped up by midnight," added the other one. The crowd **cheered**.

Barkley shook his head.

I don't see how they've nearly cracked it. They've just been signing autographs all day, while we've been doing all the work.

Come back tomorrow, folks!

The Top Dogs will be back on the case!

And back on the court for the doubles match!

CHAPTER 8

"We need a **new** plan, and fast. We have to find this **ball thief** before the Top Dogs," said Fang. Lucky for her, Barkley had a plan and it was a good one...

"Ever heard of a **stakeout**?" said Barkley.

"Yum! I love to go **OUT** for **STEAK!** It's my favorite! But I think we really should **catch** the ball thief first..."

"Not that kind of steak! **A STAKEOUT**," Barkley said.

Fang didn't know what a stakeout was. If you're a bit like Fang, let me fill you in. A stakeout is when detectives hide very quietly and wait for the culprit to turn up and then **BAM**, they catch the crook in the act! All they needed to do was **sneak** into the storeroom and wait.

Let's do it!

"Hold your tail, Fang—**first** we need some bait."

"Are we going **fishing**? I thought we were going out for steak!" said Fang.

"I'll text Carl. Stakeouts are **serious** business; we'll need supplies. Water, snacks, a good disguise ... and the bait. He should be here in no time."

Fang and Barkley **waited** outside the Dogtown Tennis Center as the last of the crowd disappeared. Mrs. McTavish's food truck had shut up shop, the Jack Russells had left for the day, and the **dog sweepers** were arriving to clean up.

Then, suddenly, a **strange** sight appeared. Two **GIANT** tennis balls came rolling toward them...

Fang's fur stood on end. It was the **stuff of nightmares**!

Fang was just about to hightail it out of there when one of the **giant balls** started calling her name.

Hey! Fang! Barkley!

AHHH!

Fang was relieved.

"Great disguise, Underdogs! You've really **outdone** yourselves this time," said Barkley.

"Did you **bounce** here from the office?" Fang asked.

"We tried to get on a bus but we **couldn't** fit through the doors!" replied Carl.

"Do you like these **disguises** for the stakeout?" Dr. Spots said as she **pulled** herself out of the ball suit. "No one will ever suspect you're in there!"

Dr. Spots had a point. Even Barkley didn't **recognize** them in those outfits.

"And who knows, the **ball thief** might even try and steal you!" added Carl.

I think he'd have a hard time stealing us, Carl!

"I agree. We'd be far **too big** for the thief to **smuggle** us out of here! What we really need is a tennis ball; that's what the ball thief loves, and there's not a single one of those **left** in Dogtown," said Barkley.

"That's why I **made** you one! Just the right size for a tennis-ball thief," Carl said, handing over a ball made of **rubber bands**!

Fang gave it a bounce.

Don't bounce it! I've planted our tracking device in there, just in case.

BOING!

126

Barkley smiled. The Underdogs were on the case! This is what being a **detective** was all about. If that ball thief was out there, tonight was the night the Underdogs were going to catch that **crook**.

"One more thing, we've got this **broken** security camera," said Barkley. "It probably didn't catch anything, but do you think you can take a look at it, Spots?"

Barkley **handed** the camera to Spots. She turned it over.

"It's old technology, and there's a big crack in it, but I might be able to get **something** off it back at the lab. I'll text you as soon as I do."

"OK, Underdogs," said Barkley, climbing into the ball. "We get just **one shot** at this. It's time to crack this case."

CHAPTER 9

Now, you might think a stakeout sounds kind of fun. You get to stay up **late** with a bag of snacks, waiting to catch a crook, but actually, it's kind of **boring**. First of all, you can't really chat or play video games, you can't yodel or scratch your butt. You need to stay sharp because at **any** minute, there could be a clue. So that's what the Underdogs did. Fang and Barkley **waddled** into the storeroom, carefully avoiding the security dogs.

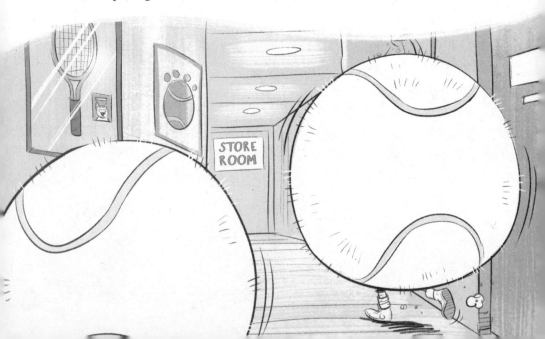

Once inside, they **planted** the rubber-band ball on the table where the ball thief would see it.

"I wish we could eat a few of those **cakes** while we wait for the ball thief to show up," said Fang, eyeing the snacks table. No such luck. She was **stuck** in that ball with a **small** bag of fish chips and that's it.

Time moves **slowly** when you're stuck inside giant tennis balls with nothing to do but eat bags of fish chips. Just ask Barkley, he **hates** fish chips!

They **watched** the door, waiting for any signs the ball thief would strike, but nothing happened.

Fang and Barkley were beginning to get tired. Very tired.

Barkley drifted off, **dreaming** of bones and sticks. And mice and balls of string began to **dance** in Fang's head.

It must have been morning when Fang was **startled** by Barkley's phone.

"It's a **message** from Spots!" whispered Barkley.

"Fang! Spots has got something off the camera! It looks like Bjorn Dawg leaving this **storeroom**. He's **hiding** something **big** under his coat! He must be our ball thief!"

"But why would he **steal** tennis balls?!" hissed Fang. "He already holds the record for the **most** Grand Slams!"

The Underdogs **gasped**. That was just it. If Barry Barker won the Grand Slam this year, then he would **break** Bjorn's record!

"Bjorn Dawg must be trying to **stop** him from winning by stealing all the tennis balls in Dogtown!" said Barkley.

Suddenly, Barkley's ears **twitched**. What was that? There it was again! It was the sound of **footsteps**, and they were getting closer. The Underdogs went quiet.

The door **creaked** open, and who do you think came sneaking in? Yup. Bjorn Dawg. He looked around the storeroom. Then his eyes **locked** on the rubber-band ball.

Ahh, a ball!

Barkly couldn't believe it. This was exactly what they had hoped for: they were about to catch the ball thief in the act. **Game. Set. Match.**

Then, suddenly, the storeroom door **slammed** shut and everything went dark! Someone had switched off the lights. There was a **rumble** and some **clanking**, then **banging** and footsteps before the door opened again and someone **ran** right out of the room.

"Come on!" shouted Fang. "We can **catch** him!"

Fang and Barkley barreled their way out of the storeroom, **banging** into things, **tripping** over equipment, only to get **stuck** in the doorway. They **scrambled** and **pushed**, but their big ball costumes made it impossible to budge.

"I'm trying!" yelled Barkley, and suddenly the pressure **shot** them both out and sent them **bouncing** down the hallway.

The **giant** balls bounced and sprang off the walls, sending them right out onto **center court**.

The morning crowd was already beginning to arrive and was waiting for the first game to start. A big **cheer** went up as the two huge balls of Fang and Barkley were **flung** onto the court. And who do you think was warming up, getting ready for their first match? Yup, that's right, the Top Dogs!

"**AHHH!**" shrieked Fang as they sped toward the startled Weimaraners!

But Bjorn was **nowhere** to be seen.

CHAPTER 10

"Don't worry! The Underdogs are on the case!" yelled Barkley as they rolled out of the tennis center and straight into a tree. **BANG!** The knock was enough to dislodge the Underdogs from their ball costumes and the two detectives **crawled** out.

They looked around. The **food trucks** and **stalls** had already started to set up and the morning crowd was still **pouring** in to see the first matches of the day. There were dogs everywhere, but **where** was the ball thief?

How will we find him now?

Fang and Barkley **headed** back over to where they'd parked their tricycle, but when they got there, something was **different**. The tracking device Spots had added to the handlebars was **lit up** like a Christmas tree.

Fang and Barkley **jumped** onto their tricycle and hit the pedals. The tracking device sent the Underdogs this way and that. First, they headed **straight** back toward town and over the Golden Retriever Bridge.

Then they **spun** along the Wagtail River where the dog markets sell everything from **antique** bones to **vintage** water bowls.

The tracker **suddenly** sent them right, and then right again.

"Is this thing broken?!" yelled Fang. "We're headed back the way we came! There's the tennis center!" They were right back **outside** the tennis center where they'd started … but the tracker wasn't broken. Right near the snack stand Fang **spotted** one very **guilty-looking** dog trying to hide … Bjorn Dawg!

Barkley tried to stop, but he couldn't. "I'm having trouble **stopping** this thing!" he yelled. He pulled the handlebars and **swerved** through the crowd, **skidding** through the security gates.

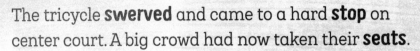

The tricycle **swerved** and came to a hard **stop** on center court. A big crowd had now taken their **seats**.

"We're **not** the entertainment," said Barkley. "We're the Underdogs and we've **cracked the case**. We know **who** the ball thief is. Follow us."

Steffi and the crowd followed the Underdogs back toward the stalls and food trucks. Bjorn Dawg was still trying to **hide** near a snack van.

"There he is!" said Barkley.

"Bjorn Dawg is the thief?!" gasped Steffi.

"I'm sorry!" said Bjorn, his **pockets** still bulging. "I just couldn't **help** myself."

At that same moment, the Top Dogs appeared.

"Oh yeah, we've **totally** cracked the case. The ball thief is Bjorn Dawg!"

The crowd began to **clap**. Bjorn Dawg looked **terribly embarrassed**.

STOP! Bjorn Dawg is not the thief!

"Sure he is!" said the Top Dogs. "We **always** crack the case."

"Not this time. Bjorn might have a **weakness**, but it's not for tennis balls. It's for **snacks**. Right, Bjorn?"

Bjorn **nodded** and emptied his pockets. **SNACKS!** Bone-flavored crisps, meaty bites, liver chews, and marrow cupcakes.

Bjorn was not the ball thief!

"When he **snuck** into the storeroom, it wasn't to **steal** the balls—it was to **gobble** snacks!" said Barkley.

"Exactly. He didn't even know the ball was there beforehand!" said Fang. "Only a dog who can **sniff** out a ball **anywhere** would have found it."

"Exactly. And the ball thief has **hidden** those balls right under our noses!" said Fang, pointing to the grass they were **standing** on.

"Wait!" yelled the Top Dogs. "Nice try, Underpants."

"It's Underdogs," **growled** Barkley. But the Top Dogs weren't paying attention.

The balls can't be buried here. This whole area has been searched and we would have sniffed them out.

"Yes," said Fang. "Unless they've been **buried** under something **soooooooooo** stinky that you can't even smell them!"

All heads **spun** and faced Mrs. McTavish's food truck. What was she making today? **Curry anchovy soup**. Yup, that will do it.

The Underdogs started **digging** a hole under the soup truck, and what do you think they found?

Get away from my van!

Tennis balls! Hundreds and **hundreds** of tennis balls! The crowd **cheered**. The Dogtown Grand Slam was **saved**. But which one of the ball dogs was responsible?

Fang was just about to point out the **culprit** when Jack Russell **stepped** forward, removing his ball-dog badge and handing it to Steffi.

"Why did you do it?" asked Steffi.

"I just **love** tennis balls! I love **catching** them. I love **chasing** them … and I love **burying** them. I guess I got a bit carried away. I'm really sorry for the **trouble** I've caused."

156

Steffi Gruff looked at the **shiny** badge and handed it back to Jack. "I'm sure you can set things right, because there's **a lot** of work to do," said Steffi.

Jack Russell **smiled**. He was up for it, particularly if that work involved **tennis balls**!

"Just one question," said Jack Russell, turning to the Underdogs. "How did you **know** it was me?"

"When you went off to look for new balls, you came back with **dirty paws** and smelling **stinky**. And nothing in Dogtown smells **that** bad ... except Mrs. McTavish's soup," said Fang.

I know what you're thinking. It's great that the Underdogs cracked the case of the **missing balls**, but **what about** the missing hedgehog? Remember Benson Henson? The Underdogs **hadn't** forgotten about him either.

It turns out they had cracked that case, too. You see, Jack Russell explained how he didn't mean to **ruin** the Grand Slam. It turns out he was just one of those dogs that had a real case of **tennis-ball-itis**. You know, when a dog just gets so ball-obsessed they **can't** think of **anything else**? Well that's what happened to poor Jack Russell.

To set things right, he had to **dig up** and **wash** hundreds of tennis balls. Jack was only too happy to get to work.

But as he started **digging** up the balls from under the soup truck, they all heard a **sound** ...

A strange **squeaking** sound, and it was coming from one very dirty-looking tennis ball.

Jack pushed the ball over to Barkley... **OUCH!** It was a spiky ball! Actually, it **wasn't** a ball at all! At least, it wasn't a tennis ball. It was Benson Henson! He'd **rolled** himself into a ball, just like hedgehogs do when they want to **hide**.

Benson **uncurled** himself and **dusted** himself off.

"Daddy!" squealed the two little hoglets **running** from the crowd.

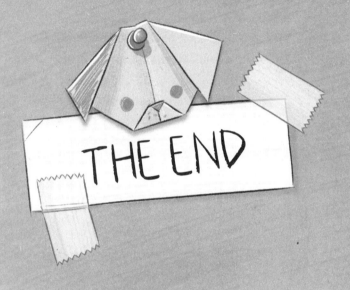

THE END

DO **YOU** HAVE WHAT IT TAKES TO BE AN **UNDERDOG** DETECTIVE?

SEARCH & FIND

A good detective can find hidden evidence. Can you find these ten words in the below grid?

**TENNIS COMMENTATOR PICTURE EXPENSIVE OPERATION
TINKERING HEDGEHOG SUSPICIOUS NEWSPAPER FLEAS**

```
R  W  N  D  V  Z  X  I  G  E  E  G  S  O  A
R  A  A  M  T  Y  Q  Q  O  K  R  G  I  P  C
S  M  G  N  R  B  K  P  R  O  L  I  N  E  L
P  U  R  E  Z  P  I  C  T  U  R  E  N  R  S
J  K  O  D  X  B  W  A  P  T  W  D  E  A  P
Z  L  Z  I  K  P  T  G  I  M  S  E  T  T  R
I  K  I  T  C  N  E  N  G  A  C  A  T  I  E
G  Q  H  A  E  I  K  N  E  T  K  R  P  O  P
M  G  L  M  C  E  P  L  S  A  G  X  J  N  A
E  R  M  Z  R  J  F  S  N  I  L  J  O  Q  P
B  O  O  I  T  T  L  X  U  J  V  Z  Q  H  S
C  T  N  T  V  R  X  S  Q  S  E  E  G  J  W
Y  G  E  A  G  G  A  U  I  S  Q  B  O  J  E
G  O  H  E  G  D  E  H  G  P  R  Q  H  P  N
B  P  K  U  Y  E  W  S  L  D  B  A  O  F  J
```

WORD SCRAMBLE

A good detective uses clues to solve a mystery. Can you complete the below sentence by unscrambling the ten clues?

If the Underdogs hadn't solved the case, the Dogtown Grand Slam would have been a _ _ _ - _ _ _ _ _ _ _ _.

KCETAR	_ _ O _ _ _
ADGGTE	_ O _ _ _ _
YECRCTIL	O _ _ _ _ _ _ _
DAIUMST	_ _ O _ _ _ _
CEUYTISR	O _ _ _ _ _ _ _
TORUCS	_ _ _ _ O _
HCIPCMIOR	_ _ _ O _ _ _ _ _
OXANSTIUHE	_ _ _ _ _ _ _ _ O _
OCTSPASERT	_ O _ _ _ _ _ _ _ _
BDHADAEN	O O _ _ _ _ _ _

SPOT THE DIFFERENCE

A good detective knows when something is out of place. Can you find the ten differences between these two pictures?

ANSWER KEY

So how did you do?

SEARCH & FIND

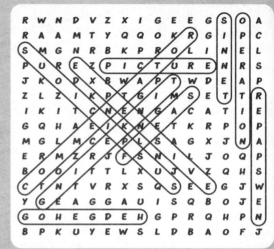

R W N D V Z X I G E E G S O A
R A A M T Y Q Q O K R G I P C
S M G N R B K P R O L I N E L
P U R E Z P I C T U R E N R S
J K O D X B W A P T W D E A P
Z L Z I K P T G I M S E T I E
I K I T C N E W G A C A T O R
G Q H A E I K N E T K R P N E
M G L M C E P S A G X J N A P
E R M Z R J F S N I L J O Q P
B O O I T T L X U J V Z Q H S
C T N T V R X S G S E E G J W
Y G E A G G A U I S Q B O J E
G O H E G D E H G P R Q H P N
B P K U Y E W S L D B A O F J

WORD SCRAMBLE

Racket, Gadget, Tricycle, Stadium, Security, Courts, Microchip, Exhaustion, Spectators, Headband

Answer to the clues: *Cat*-astrophe!

SPOT THE DIFFERENCE

*If you speak to Carl, hang up and call back until someone else answers.

CRIME IS ON THE RISE IN DOGTOWN, AND IT'S ALL THANKS TO A GUITAR BANDIT!

DogAid, the hottest music festival in town, has arrived, but Mick Wagger's lucky golden guitar has gone missing. Could one of Mick's biggest fans—the Boneheads—be behind it? Or a fellow rockstar like Justin Beaver or Catty Perry? No matter who the culprit is, if they're not stopped, the festival will be ruined, and no one will get to see The Rolling Bones hit the stage.

So it's time to call in the Underdog Detective Agency! Will they be able to stop the thief and save the show? If not, they may end up in deep treble.